missy violet and me

missy violet and me

BY BARBARA HATHAWAY

Houghton Mifflin Company
Boston

www.houghtonmifflinbooks.com

The text of this book is set in 12-point Granjon.

Library of Congress Cataloging-in-Publication Data

Hathaway, Barbara, 1944–
Missy Violet and me / by Barbara Hathaway.
p. cm.

Summary: During the early 1900s, eleven-year-old Viney spends her summer
working for the local midwife and learns firsthand about birth, death, and
"catchin' babies."
HC ISBN: 978-0-618-37163-1
PB ISBN: 978-0-618-80919-6
[1. Midwives—Fiction. 2. Birth—Fiction. 3. African Americans—Fiction.] I.
Title.
PZ7.H2819Mi 2004
[Fic]—dc22

2003017700

Manufactured in the United States of America
HAD 10 9 8 7 6 5 4 3 2 1

This book is dedicated to the memory of my loving mother, Viney Eleanor Steele, who first told me about Missy Violet. And to my aunts, Carrie Joyner and Lillie Spence.

Also, to the caring nurse midwives of the Columbia Presbyterian Medical Center, with whom I worked from 1989 to 1993. To the memory of the real Missy Violet. And to midwives everywhere.

❧ ACKNOWLEDGMENTS ❧

Special Thanks

To my kind daughter, Jacqueline Doyle Teague, who supported me every inch of the way and who wouldn't let me give up. To my granddaughter, Erica Nicole, who helped me keep my sense of humor. To my gentle father, Bennie Steele, who always believed I could do this.

To Mr. Frank Desilvestro, author of *Songs and Stories Children Love*. And to Professor Virginia Scott of Lehman College. To Gabriella Lynch and Diana Patnik. To Sylvia Frazier and Yvonne Spanne. And to all those who were rooting for me.

And a special, special thanks to Kate O'Sullivan, for guidance and for helping me pull it all together.

To Matthew Webb of Peckham Industries—thank you for rescuing me.

MISSY VIOLET

WHEN I WAS ELEVEN YEARS OLD, MY MAMA GAVE birth to her seventh child, a baby girl named Cleo. I remember it clear as yesterday because I rode in the wagon with Papa that dark, rainy night and held the lantern for him while he drove to get Missy Violet, the midwife.

Later on that night, a new baby came to our house. And after she was all tucked away in bed with Mama, Papa and Missy Violet sat and talked for a long time by the fire. I crept down to the foot of the bed and strained my ears so I could hear what they were saying.

Papa had a long, worried face, and he was sitting with his head bowed like he was in church. He said it was a bad time for the baby to come, with work being slow at the tobacco factory and with him having to pay book rent for all six of us to attend school. "I'm not gonna be able to come up with your fee for the baby this time," Papa told Missy Violet.

"You still owe me for the last one, James," Missy Violet answered. I know this made Papa sad, because my Papa, he's a very proud man and nothing bothers him worse than not being able to pay what he owes. He always pays his debts, even if he has to pay with eggs, chickens, or collard greens. So Missy Violet gave him an idea.

"Why don't you let Savanah work for me this summer, James?" she asked. Savanah is my big sister; she's seventeen. Papa started to pull on his chin, the way he does whenever he's thinking real hard about something.

Finally he said, "To tell you the truth, Missy Violet, I need Savanah here to help out around the house."

"What about Viney, then?" Missy Violet suggested. "She's getting to be a big girl." When I heard my name, my ears began to tingle and I tried to stretch them the way our dog, Goldie, stretches hers whenever she hears something out in the woodshed.

"Well, I don't know," Papa said, scratching his chin and screwing up his face.

"She's not hardheaded, is she?" Missy Violet wanted to know.

"No, she's not hardheaded. But she's a little kittenish, and sometimes I have to scold her. But mostly she's a good girl and she minds."

"You sure, now?" Missy Violet asked. "I need somebody who'll do exactly like I say."

"She'll mind you," Papa said.

Missy Violet slapped her hands together. "It's all set then!" she cried. "She can start as soon as school is out."

Some of the wrinkles fell out of Papa's forehead, but his face still looked a little sad. "It's a deal then," he said and shook Missy Violet's hand.

I could hardly wait for school to be out. Missy Violet was one of the most looked-up-to ladies in Richmond County. She knew how to bring babies into the world! "Baby catchin'" was her specialty. All of a sudden, I felt real important. "Gonna work for Missy Violet, work for Missy Violet!" I sang softly under my breath. "Gonna catch a baby, gonna catch a baby!" I felt like clapping my hands too, but then I remembered—I was supposed to be asleep.

MARGIE POOLE

THE ROAD TO MISSY VIOLET'S HOUSE RAN RIGHT PAST the Pooles' house. Every time I passed by, seven little Pooles would tumble out the door. "Hey, Viney!" they'd holler.

"Hey!" I'd holler back. Sometimes Margie Poole would sashay out onto the porch. Margie was their older sister. She and I were in the same grade at school, but I didn't like her very much. She was a "knoll-ya." That's short for a know-it-all. "Where do you think you're going, Miss Viney?" she asked one morning as I was walking by.

I poked my chest out and answered, "I'm on my way to help Missy Violet catch some babies, if you don't mind, Miss Margie Poole."

"Humph!" Margie snorted, all snooty-like. "I bet you don't know the first thing about babies," she said. "I bet you still think babies come out of a tree stump or a cabbage patch."

"Well, they do, don't they?" I said. And Margie Poole just laughed all high and mighty and stuck her nose up in the air and marched back in the house. Oooooooo, she made me so mad! But she was right—I didn't know a thing about babies, except that whenever Missy Violet came with her big black bag, she left a baby behind, every time. She *did* bring the babies in her bag, didn't she? And she *did* find them inside tree stumps or cabbage patches, didn't she? How else would they come into the world?

As soon as I got to Missy Violet's house, I told her what Margie Poole had said. Missy Violet just smiled a patient smile and shook her head, then a serious look came over her face. The kind of look Missus Mims, our Sunday School teacher, gets whenever she reads the Bible to us. "Viney," she said, "Margie's right, babies don't come from tree stumps or grow in cabbage patches. They grow inside their mothers' bellies and when the time is right they come out."

Well, for goodness sake! I thought. So that was why Mama's belly got so big before Cleo came. But every time I'd ask her about it, she'd just shoo me away and tell me not to ask so many questions. Then Savanah told me Mama had swallowed a lot of watermelon seeds and that that was why her belly was so big. "Why didn't someone just tell me the truth?" I asked.

Missy Violet smiled. "Sometimes folks make up silly tales to keep children from getting too wise before their time," she said.

"So, if babies come from their mothers, why do folks say that you catch them?" I asked.

"Well, the catchin' part is just a way of saying I help them come into the world. Let's just say my hands are their welcome mats."

"Missy Violet, do you think I'll get a chance to help you catch a baby this summer?" I asked.

"We'll see," Missy Violet said. "We'll see."

ROOTS AND HERBS

MISSY VIOLET'S HOUSE WAS LIKE A TREASURE CHEST, full of all kinds of curious things. Books and pictures and games, candlesticks, dolls, and photographs. There was a big white organ in the parlor, and a grandfather clock. But my favorite thing was the tall red cabinet that sat in her kitchen. It had glass doors and was filled with jars and bottles and tins and hundreds of brown paper sacks filled with bark, roots, grasses and leaves, seeds, cobwebs, and hens' feathers.

Right away Missy Violet began to teach me about herb medicine. We would go into the thick, shady part of the woods and Missy Violet would point to a plant or a flower or a leaf and say, "See that plant over there, Viney, the one with the little blue fruits and the three leaves shaped like fingers?" And I'd say, "Yes, ma'am."

Then she'd say, "Go over and touch the one I'm talking about." And I'd go over and point to the one she wanted. "That's sassafras," she'd say. "It's good for cleaning out the body." Then she'd pull up some of the plant's roots and cut them off and put them in the leather pouch she carried whenever she went into the woods.

We'd walk a little farther and she'd say, "See here, Viney," and point to a plant with fluffy white leaves. "This is horehound. It's very good for coughs. And that weed over there with the pinkish flowers and the red berries on it? That's squaw vine. It's a fine medicine for my ladies who are about to give birth.

Go ahead, touch it. Smell it. Now, let Missy Violet see you pull up some of its roots and cut them off." And I'd pull up the plant and cut some of its roots off and toss them into Missy Violet's leather pouch. Sometimes when we didn't go into the woods, we'd go in the wheat fields to find a midwife herb called shepherd's purse. The white flowers on it looked like tiny little triangle-shaped purses. Missy Violet said if she gave one of her ladies a teacupful of this herb with the juice of one orange, three times a day for a month before her baby's birth, it would make her labor easier.

The roots and herbs weren't easy to learn at first—so many different names and shapes and colors! But Missy Violet was real patient with me, and she talked to me about each one I'd learn. She believed herbs were special, a gift from God, that could help folks bear their aches and pains. We even made up a little game. As soon as we'd get back from the woods, we'd go straight to the red cabinet, and for every plant I could name without looking at the label Missy Violet would give me a penny. It wasn't long before I had a Mason jar full of coins. Enough to pay my book rent when school started.

LITTLE BENNIE SATTIFIELD COMES INTO THE WORLD

Every Monday Missy Violet boiled her sheets and packed her "birthin' bags." One of my jobs was to help her pack them. She always kept two bags ready at all times, filled with two clean, starched sheets, a clean, starched apron, a bandana, a cake of brown soap, two pairs of scissors, a skein of flannel, white shoestrings, a bottle of sweet oil, a bag of squaw-root tea, a bag of bitterweed, a small basin, a scale, receiving blankets, burlap diapers, birth records, envelopes and postage stamps, and a flask of blackberry wine.

But Missy Violet didn't deliver many babies that summer. Mostly we visited the sick and shut in, like cranky Mister Odell, who had the rheumatism so bad, he never spoke to anybody. Or like Missus Socrates, one of Missy Violet's white lady-friends who needed headache powders. Or like Missus Dockery's little girl, Maggie, who'd been born with crooked hands. Missy Violet would put little splints on her fingers and show her how to sleep with her hands tucked underneath her head so that her fingers would grow out straight.

When Missy Violet wasn't visiting the sick or gathering herbs in the woods, she was in her kitchen, baking sweetbreads and cornpones for the people she visited. Sometimes she'd let me help. I'd stir the corn and nutmeg into the eggs for the cornpones and sprinkle big, plump, juicy raisins into the bread pudding mix. Missy Violet's kitchen always smelled like a holiday.

One day while Missy Violet and I were baking, we heard someone yelling in the front yard. "Missy Violet! Missy Violet!" It was Broady Sattifield, and he was all nervous and excited.

"What's the matter, Broady?" Missy Violet called through the window.

"Papa say come quick, Mama's time done come!" Missy Violet put the fire out in the oven and grabbed her bag and a loaf of sweetbread that was cooling on the table. "Come on, Viney," she said. "We've got a baby to catch!" Missy Violet put her straw hat on and struck out walking down the road. She walked fast, and Broady and I had to skip some and run some just to keep up with her.

"You letting me help?" I asked Missy Violet as I trotted up the road.

"Of course," she said. "Don't you want to?"

I didn't know what to say because now that the time had come, I wasn't so sure. "What will I do?" I asked.

"You can keep Broady company while I deliver the baby," Missy Violet answered.

"Oh, I can do that!" I said.

On the way, we ran into the Pooles. Seven little Pooles followed us up the road, asking questions and trying to pat Missy Violet's bag.

"Hey, Missy Violet! Where you goin'? What you got in your bag? A baby?"

"Can't stop to talk now, babies," Missy Violet told them. "See you on the way back." Missy Violet called all the children in the neighborhood her babies because she had delivered most of them. And sometimes, when she came across a child being naughty, she'd scold him and say, "You listen to me, now. I brung you in the world. Now, you behave so Missy Violet won't be sorry she tended your birth."

When we got to the Sattifields', Missus Sattifield was all piled up in the bed, moaning and groaning. Missy Violet went over to the bed and said some kind words to her. "Daisy, you put your mind at ease now, honey, Missy Violet's here to help you." Then Missy Violet put a large kettle of water on the stove and put Mister Sattifield and Broady outdoors.

"Viney, I'm going to need you in here with me," Missy Violet said, and her voice had changed. It was very stern and businesslike. "You do exactly like I say, now, do you hear?" she said.

"Yes, ma'am," I answered.

Then Missy Violet took a big bar of brown lye soap out of her bag and led me over to the kitchen sink. "Viney, do you know your alphabet?"

"Yes, ma'am, I sure do!" I answered.

"Then don't stop washing your hands with this soap until you say the whole alphabet. By then your hands should be good and clean." So Missy Violet and I said the alphabet while we washed our hands, then we rinsed and rinsed and rinsed.

After the hand-washing Missy Violet went to her birthin' bag and pulled out a long white apron and put it on. "Tie it in the back for me, Viney," she said.

"Make a nice, neat bow." And I made a nice, neat bow, just the way Missy Violet had told me to. "Now," she said, "we'll make Daisy a cup of hot tea."

Missy Violet made Missus Sattifield a cup of squaw-root tea, a special tea she brewed only for her ladies who were giving birth. She said the squaw-root tea would make the babies come faster. Missus Sattifield drank the hot tea a little sip at a time. When she finished, her labor pains began to come faster, and her moans and groans got louder and louder. Missy Violet went over to the bed and laid her hands on Missus Sattifield's belly. "Things coming along just fine, Daisy," she said. Then she rubbed sweet oil all over Missus Sattifield's swollen belly.

After a while, Missus Sattifield began to ball up her fists and grit her teeth, and big veins puffed out on the sides of her head, like the big veins that popped out on Papa's head whenever he chopped wood. "Missy Violet, what's wrong with her?" I asked, all nervous-like.

"She's havin' what we call 'labor pains,'" Missy Violet explained to me. "Her body's working hard to push the baby out." Then Missy Violet took a look at my face and asked, "Viney, do you want to go home?"

It took me a little while to answer because seeing Broady's mama like that made me feel scared and sad and all at once; I *did* want to be at home with Mama and Papa. I felt shame crawling on my face like a wiggly worm, and I couldn't look at Missy Violet when I said, "Oh, I'll just go on outside and keep Broady company, ma'am."

But Broady didn't seem much in the mood for company when I got outside. He just sat on the kitchen step and wrote in the dirt with a stick. He didn't even want to talk. Maybe he was too worried about his ma. I got a stick and sat and wrote in the dirt for a while, too. I didn't feel much like playing either—I had let Missy Violet down, and after all the things she'd taught me. I hadn't meant to let her down—it was just the way Missus Sattifield had been carrying on. I think it would have been much easier if the babies *did* come out of tree stumps and cabbage patches. But then I thought about that snooty Margie Poole, and I stomped right back into the house. "Missy Violet, ma'am," I said, "tell me what you want me to do!"

"All right, then," Missy Violet said, "wash your hands and give me a clean sheet out of the black bag." Missy Violet folded the sheet over three times and made a thick pad to go underneath Missus Sattifield. "It's time," she said. "Now, Viney, you climb up on the bed and get behind Daisy."

What on earth did Missy Violet want me to do?

"Get behind the pillows and let Daisy's head rest on your shoulder. And don't you come down from behind those pillows unless I tell you to! Do you understand?" Missy Violet said in a serious, I-mean-exactly-what-I-say voice.

"Yes, ma'am," I answered, and I did everything

that I was told. But my heart was galloping like a runaway pony.

"Now, when I say PUSH! you push the pillows hard against Daisy's back," Missy Violet told me. "PUSH!" Missy Violet shouted and I pushed the pillows as hard as I could. Missus Sattifield squeezed her eyes shut and huffed and puffed and strained until her face was wet with sweat. But no baby came out. Then Missy Violet did a curious thing. She stretched herself across the bed, right across Missus Sattifield's swollen belly. "PUSH, DAISY, PUSH!" she cried.

Missus Sattifield pushed and strained some more. Then Missy Violet stood up and pressed and rubbed and kneaded Missus Sattifield's belly until sweat rolled from her head and soaked her bandana. All the while she hummed and prayed and sang. My arms started to ache and cramp from pushing so hard on the pillows, but I didn't dare let up.

All at once Missy Violet ran to the foot of the bed

and shouted, "Glory, it's comin'! I can see the crown of its little round head!" Then Missy Violet spread the palms of her hands out like a catcher's mitt and Missus Sattifield PUSHHHHHHHHHed one more time and a little baby popped out, right into Missy Violet's hands. "It's a boy!" she cried. "It's a little boy."

Missy Violet used the sterilized shoestring and scissors to tie and cut the baby's birth cord, so she could separate him from his mother. I'd helped her boil and wrap the shoestring and scissors the day before. Hot jiggetty! I bet Margie Poole didn't know a thing about boiled scissors and shoestring! All of a sudden, I didn't feel scared or dumb anymore. I felt proud and very smart.

After Missy Violet separated the baby from his mother, she cleaned him up. He squalled and wiggled the whole time she worked on him. "He got a good set of lungs, Daisy!" Missy Violet shouted over all the noise the baby was making. Then she weighed him on the funny little scale she kept in her bag. "What a fine boy," she said. "Almost ten pounds. What's his name, Daisy?"

"Bennie, ma'am," Missus Sattifield said, "After my papa."

"Little Bennie, you now in the world!" Missy Violet said as she wrapped a piece of flannel around the baby's middle to hold his little belly button in place. After that she wrapped him up in a blanket, gave him a hug, and handed him to his mother. Missus Sattifield chuckled and cooed and talked to the baby while Missy Violet made her comfortable.

"Hi, little Bennie," I said, over Missus Sattifield's shoulder, but the little baby had gone fast asleep. He wasn't pretty and smooth like my baby sister, Cleo, had been when she was born. He was all red and wrinkly and tired-looking. He didn't favor the Sattifields at all, but there was something sweet and cute about him just the same. "Viney, you can come down off the bed now," Missy Violet said, and I climbed down off of the pile of pillows.

In the kitchen Missy Violet made coffee and sliced up the sweetbread she'd brought. "Viney, you are smart and strong. You're a fine helper," she said and gave me a big hug. "Now, you go tell Mister Sattifield and Broady it's all right to come back inside while I fill out this birth record to send to the county seat." As I walked to the door, I felt a great big wide grin spreading across my face.

On the way back home, we ran into the Pooles again. "Oh, *Marrr*-gie," I sang as we passed by. "I just helped Missy Violet catch a baby." Margie just shrugged her shoulders and her eyebrows like she didn't even care. But I didn't mind. I was sure I knew more about "catchin' babies" than she did.

And more important, Papa's debt was paid.

CHARLES ELISTER PAXTON NEHEMIAH WINDBUSH

BETWEEN THE TIME I HELPED MISSY VIOLET CATCH little Bennie Sattifield and the time school started, my cousin Charles came down from Mt. Gilead. His mama had been feeling poorly, so Papa said he could go to school down here with us until things got better at home. The only trouble was that Charles stirred up mischief everywhere he went. He was a real cutup. You'd think with a name like Charles Elister Paxton Nehemiah Windbush he'd behave himself. But instead he just got under everybody's skin, including mine.

"A scamp!" "A real botheration!" "A bad egg!" That's what folks called him behind his back. Some folks believed he was the way he was because of his red hair. "A red-headed Negro is sure enough kin to the devil," they'd say. And whenever we'd go by, they'd point and whisper, "There goes the devil's stepson!" And sometimes I believed they were right.

But Papa said that that was just foolish talk. That Charles's hair was red because he took after old man Elister Russell, his part-Irish great-granddaddy on his mama's side. Mama said Charles behaved the way he did because his mama and his papa had "spared the rod and spoiled the child" just like the Good Book said. And that what he needed was a good shellackin' with a hickory switch.

The only time I can remember Charles behaving himself was when he was around Missy Violet. Maybe that was because Missy Violet never scolded him and always made over his red hair. I guess she felt sorry for him, because his mama was sick and all.

Sometimes the two of us would slip down to her house for a visit and she'd make us feel right at home, clucking over us like a mother hen. She'd stuff us with goodies and let us play games and look at photographs. And if we were very good and didn't fuss and fight, she'd let us play a tune on the fancy white organ that sat in her parlor.

Charles thought he was hot stuff on that organ, and Missy Violet didn't help his swollen head any by telling him he'd be a fine musician some day. I just hated when she did that, because Charles would get all biggity and mannish and try to boss me around for the rest of the day. Besides, I couldn't see how he'd ever be a real musician. Real musicians had to keep plenty of tunes and notes in their heads. Charles could only keep devilment in his head, and he couldn't deliver a message from his pinky to his thumb without getting it all jumbled up.

Like the time Mama sent him to poor, addle-brained Miss Liza Little with some laundry bluing.

Mama told Charles to tell Miss Liza to put the bluing in her rinse water so her linens would come out white and bright. But Charles told Miss Liza that Mama said to put the bluing in her "drinkin' water," and poor Miss Liza did just that. And came to prayer meeting that night with her mouth all blue!

Charles told Mama he was sorry, but I didn't believe him. I think he did it on purpose.

Sometimes when we went to visit Missy Violet, we'd sit on the front porch and sip lemonade while she'd tell us how things used to be back in slavery time, when she was a little girl. How when she was only seven years old the Union soldiers came from "up North" and seized her master's plantation. Missy Violet said they came early one morning, while it was still dark and everyone was in bed. They rounded up all the slaves and marched them up to the master's big front lawn. Then she said a Yankee soldier, with a wide hat and a beard the color of iron, stepped up on the veranda and pulled out a long, important-looking piece of paper. "It was the longest piece of paper my young eyes had ever seen," Missy Violet told us.

The paper was called the *Emancipation Proclamation,* and it had been signed by the president of the United States himself, Mister Abraham Lincoln. "Can you imagine that, children!" Missy Violet laughed. The paper said that all the slaves had been set free.

When the slaves heard that they were free, Missy Violet said they began to whoop and holler and dance because they were so glad. "Never heard such shoutin' and singin' and ringin' of the cow bells in all my born days as I heard on that day," she told us. She said that some of the old slaves were so grateful that they got down on their knees and kissed the stripe on the side of the Yankee soldier's navy blue britches. "Even I was jumpin' up and down and clappin' my hands, though I didn't understand what it was all about. But there I was," Missy Violet said, "standing there, takin' it all in through my seven-year-old eyes."

And every time Missy Violet told us that story, her eyes would shine and shine and shine, like brand-new silver money.

The Rausy Brothers

Some afternoons after school was over, Charles and I would run errands for Missy Violet. They were usually to some more sick and shut-ins, like Mister Johnnie Browne, who suffered so badly with the weeping eczema that he needed polk-root salve to rub on his body just so he could bear to have his clothes on. Or to Miss Roula Olette, who had tired blood and poor circulation and needed boneset tonic to make her feel better.

About once a month, we'd deliver a small tin of

Tube Rose snuff to Miss Ida Bean, a real old, old lady everyone called Missus Methuselah because she was older than anyone else in the county. Folks said she'd been born in bondage and was already forty-five years old when freedom came. So that made her over one hundred years old!

Miss Ida's crinkley hair was white as snow, and her dark skin was wrinkled and leathery like Papa's old travelin' bag. Most times when we came up on her porch, she wouldn't say a word. But as soon as we handed her her tin of snuff, she'd scour some on her gums with a peach twig and start humming a little tune that sounded like "Blue Tail Fly." Then she'd say, "Chil'lun, y'all know your scriptures?" And we'd say, "Yes, ma'am. 'Blessed are the meek.'" Then she'd smile and tell us, "Mind your mama." And we'd answer, "Yes, ma'am," and she'd go back to humming her tune. And that was all she ever said to us.

Sometimes when we took Miss Ida her snuff,

we'd tote a jug of blackberry wine up the hill to Miss Sarah Bright's house. Miss Bright was a real old lady too, but not as old as Miss Ida. Folks said she used to own slaves and kept the coach whip she used to beat them with up over the fireplace in her parlor.

Every time we went up the hill to her house, Charles would get all biggity and say how he was going to walk right up to Miss Bright and ask her about that coach whip. But as soon as we'd step up on the porch and Miss Bright would look at him with her pale blue eyes that looked like two hard chunks of blue ice, Charles would lose all his gumption. "Well, what's the matter with ya, boy? Set the jug down!" Miss Bright would snap, and I'd nudge Charles and say, "Go ahead, ask her 'bout the coach whip." But he'd just stand there with his knees knocking until Miss Bright would start pounding her walking stick on the porch and hissing like a rattlesnake. And Charles would take off running down the hill! Then Miss Bright would wink at me and we'd both laugh at Charles running away like a little red ant.

But the errand I hated going on the most was to the Rausy brothers'. The Rausy brothers were as crazy as two road lizards and lived all alone, way down in the woods near a swamp—in a place everybody called The Fork.

The year my cousin Charles came to stay with us, the Rausy brothers caught a bad case of the "seven-year itch." That was a rash that was so hard to get rid of, folks said it took up to seven years to go away.

Once Missy Violet sent us out to the Rausy brothers' with a big tin of polk-root salve. "Just set it down on the porch and leave, children," Missy Violet had instructed us. But when we got there, Charles, who thought the Rausy brothers were better than a three-ring circus, pushed the door wide open and hollered inside. "HEY! RAUSY, HAUSY BROTHERS, C'MON OUT!"

Pax, the one with the peculiar-looking, lopsided head and the voice that sounded like two paper sacks being rubbed together, shuffled out first. Then Bledsoe, the one with the big yellow teeth and the herky-jerky laugh, came out behind him. "TELL US A HAINT STORY!" Charles shouted, then cut his eye at me and grinned because he loved to see me get all crazy-scared whenever anybody told a scary story.

I wanted to leave Charles right there on that broken-down porch, but I didn't relish going back through the woods by myself. "C'MON, TELL US A STORY!" Charles squawked, his eyes all shiny and greedy-looking.

So the one named Pax said in his scratchy, scary voice: "Did you hear that, Brer' Bledsoe? These here scamps wanna hear a haint story."

Bledsoe clenched his big yellow teeth together and laughed his herky-jerky laugh. *"Hic-a, hic-a, hic-a, hic-a, heeeeeeeeeeeeeeeeeeeeee!"*

"Reckon I oughta' tell 'em 'bout Hairy Esau?" Pax asked.

And Bledsoe said through his big crooked teeth, "Yes, sir-reeee-de-bob, Brer' Pax. You tell 'em 'bout Hairy Esau."

"Yeah, yeah! Tell us 'bout Hairy Esau!" Charles kept shouting.

"Well, 'twas like this," Pax said. "An ol' farmer by the name of Esau got all rigged out in his huntin' outfit and went out and bagged hisself a sight of game. He come back through the woods that evenin', all tired and give out like a old mule, wit some rabbits and squirrels and possums throwed across his shoulders.

"Now, don't you know, ol' Esau stepped in a hole in the ground and fell to the bottom faster 'n a barrel full of nails!" When Pax said "faster 'n a barrel full of nails," Bledsoe began to howl and laugh like it was the funniest thing he'd ever heard. And he kept up that herky-jerky laughing for the longest time. Just like Uncle Oll did when the men in the white coats came down from Goldsboro to cart him off to the rest home.

"It was dark down in that hole," Pax went on, "and poor ol' Esau tried like the devil to get out. He hollered and hollered, but nobody heard him. Finally he hollered so long, his voice plum give out and all he could do was whisper 'Hep, hep, get me outta here!'

"His hair growed all the way down to his waist, and his toenails and fingernails growed long and crooked like buzzard claws. Finally ol' Esau lay down and died.

"Way by and by, some hunters come across ol' Esau down in the hole, so they carted ol' Esau off to the graveyard and whittled on his tombstone 'Here lies Hairy Esau.'

"Now, you know, haints don't walk unlessin' they got somethin' troublin' their minds. And ol' Esau's ghost wanted to get back to that hole to see if anybody been botherin' 'round wit his game. So every time the moon stand low, Hairy Esau's ghost creep out in the woods and watch that hole."

All of a sudden, Bledsoe hollered, "Brer' Pax, Brer' Pax, ain't the moon gon' be standin' low tonight?"

"I believe you right 'bout that, Brer' Bledsoe," Pax answered. "You scamps best be gettin' along. Moon be comin' out soon and ol' Esau be skulkin' 'round out there in them woods, lookin' for his hole. Sometime he be waitin' down in the hole, waitin' for a little scamp to come along through the woods. He be real quiet down there, then he'll reach up and grab that little scamp by the ankle and down he go!"

"Yeah," said Bledsoe, "they say he snatched a woman and a whole passel of chil'lun down that hole one night. *Hic-a, hic-a, hic-a, heeeeeeeeeeeee.*"

"Y'all ever seen him?" my brazen cousin Charles asked.

"Why, sho' we has!" squawked Bledsoe. "Ain't we, Brer' Pax?"

"Done seen him plenty-a times," answered Pax. "Brer' Bledsoe, you remember the time he got at us? Run us clean outten our britches, didn't he! Scared us so bad, Brer' Bledsoe's hair riz up."

"Come on, Charles, the sun goin' down," I whispered. But Charles wouldn't budge. He had to ask one more question. "Does he say anything?" he asked.

"He sho' do," answered Pax.

"Well, what does he say?"

"Well, he say somethin' different every time, that's all," said Bledsoe. "Depend on what mood he in. Sometime he say somethin' nice like, 'Them sho' is nice shoes you got on.' Or he might say somethin' like, 'I'm gwine fix yo business good, you devilish scamp!' Or maybe he say, 'I'm gwine wreak havoc on you, you miserable backslider . . . I seen what you done!' All depends on what mood he in."

"When he got after me and Brer' Bledsoe, he musta' been in a real ugly humor," said Pax, "'cause, he hollered, 'I'm gwine jar yo heads loose!' Then he tried to grab me and Brer' Bledsoe by the ankles. But Brer' Bledsoe kept hollerin', 'Lay down body! Lay down body!' 'Cause that's what you suppose to say when a haint get after you and then he'll turn you loose."

"Hic-a, hic-a, hic-a, heeeeeeeeeeeeeeeeeee," Bledsoe laughed.

All of a sudden, the Rausy brothers cocked their heads toward the woods. "Listen!" hissed Pax.

"Sound like Hairy Esau's long toenails scrapin' the ground right now, don't it, Brer' Bledsoe?"

"I declare, it sho' do," answered Bledsoe. Then all of a sudden, while we were still standing there with our mouths open, those mean ol' Rausy brothers shoved us off the porch and slammed the door behind us! They didn't even say goodbye. Charles and I scampered through the woods like two wild billy goats, flinching and jerking all the way home, yelling, "LAY DOWN BODY! LAY DOWN BODY!" Because we thought every noise or sound and every leaf that moved was Hairy Esau coming out of the ground to snatch us down to the bottom of a hole, faster than a barrel full of nails!

That night in bed, I had to stare myself to sleep, looking up at the ceiling, because every time I closed my eyes, I could see Hairy Esau and the Rausy brothers all coming at me in the dark. And I could hear Bledsoe's herky-jerky laugh, *"hic-a, hic-a, hic-a,"* all night long in my head.

I could hardly wait for Charles's mama to get better so he could go back home.

MISTER JOE BRICK'S TWINS

IT WAS TIME FOR MISTER JOE BRICK'S EIGHTH BABY
to be born, but he was too ashamed to send for Missy
Violet because he still owed her for delivering his
last seven babies. So it was Missus Brick who sent
for Missy Violet when her time came. When Missy
Violet got there, Missus Brisk was all frightened and
worried and she thanked Missy Violet over and over
again for coming. She said something just didn't
seem right about this baby and she was one to know
because she had birthed seven babies, just like my
mama had.

Missy Violet laid her hands on Missus Brick's belly and pressed. "Baby movin' around in there just fine," Missy Violet told her. But then a puzzled look spread over Missy Violet's face, and she kept pressing Missus Brick's belly with her fingers, around and around in a circle. "Hmmm, that's curious," she said.

"What's wrong?" Missus Brick asked.

"Not sure," Missy Violet answered. "But keep up your courage; Missy Violet's here to help you all she can," she said. Then Missy Violet hurried out to the kitchen to make Missus Brick a cup of her special tea.

"Now, Viney, you stay in the front room and entertain these children while I tend to Darsenior," Missy Violet said to me as she walked through the parlor to the kitchen. When she got to the kitchen door she turned around and said, "And whatever you do, don't let them young'uns in the bedroom." Then she said to Missus Brick's children, "Now, you babies content yourselves in here with Viney. Do you hear me?" And all the little Brick children said, "Yes, ma'am." I said, "Yes, ma'am" too, but I wanted to get in that bedroom with Missy Violet to watch her work her magic and bring a brand-new baby into the world. After all, hadn't Missy Violet told me that I was her best helper girl?

The Brick children were like seven little stairsteps, each one just a teensy bit taller than the other. Folks even called them "Brick's Stairsteps." They crawled all over me like picnic ants, asking questions and begging for things. "Biney, what yo mama name?" "How old you is?" "Gib' us a biscuit." "Weed us a stor'wee." "Gib us a piggy-back ride."

I did everything I could to charm those little wiggly-worms, but they just wouldn't keep still. But every chance I got, I meandered over by the bedroom door to see if I could hear what was going on inside. And the little Brick children would say "Oooooh, Biney, you near the bedroom!" Finally I heard Missy Violet say, "It's crownin'! Bear down hard, girl!" And I knew that meant the baby was about to come out.

Just then, the little Brick named Willie, the one who picked his nose all the time, said, "Let's doe outside."

"No!" I said. "I have to stay in here in case Missy Violet needs me to help."

"Help do what?" Pearl, the oldest girl asked.

"Catch the baby," I said.

"Catch a baby?"

"Why, sure," I said and tried to make my voice sound all grown up and important, the way my oldest brother, James Dallas, did whenever the young courtin' girls gathered around him on the church grounds.

Then all of a sudden, we heard a baby cry and the door flew open. "Viney, come tend this baby. We not done in here yet!" Missy Violet called, in her stern, businesslike voice.

"Yes, ma'am," I answered, and told the Brick children to sit down and be still. "If one of you moves, somethin' bad is gonna happen to you," I told them. And their little eyes got as round as wagon wheels and Willie started pickin' his nose, but they all stayed right where I left them while I went in the bedroom to help Missy Violet.

The room was hot and stuffy inside, and a little squallin' baby lay on the bed, squirming in a blanket. Missy Violet said, "Viney, pick that baby up and go sit in that chair over there by the window, and don't you move, child, unless I tell you to."

So I did just as I was told and picked up the baby and held her tight so she wouldn't slip out of my arms and went over to the chair by the window. She must have liked the way I was holding her because she stopped squallin' and settled down. But I noticed that Missy Violet wasn't making Missus Brick comfortable yet, the way she'd made Missus Sattifield comfortable after little Bennie came out. But she kept right on working on Missus Brick.

All at once, Missy Violet cried, "I do declare!"

"Lordy, what is it?" cried Missus Brick.

"Looks like you had two biscuits in the oven this

time, Darsenior. You about to get yourself a set of twins."

"Twins!" squawked Missus Brick.

"Bear down good and hard one more time and it'll be over," Missy Violet told her. So Missus Brick gritted her teeth and beared down real hard and a second little baby popped out, right into Missy Violet's hands, just like little Bennie had!

But this little baby didn't move or squall, or suck his fists. He just lay there all puny and kind of blue, like a sick puppy. Missy Violet picked the poor little fellow up and started to rub his back and chest. Then she began to talk and sing into his tiny little ear. Next she wrapped him in a blanket and walked around the room with him in her arms, talking and rubbing and singing until the little baby let out a sad little sound like a baby lamb would make.

"Is he gonna be all right?" Missus Brick asked.

"I believe he'll come around," Missy Violet said and laid the baby in Missus Brick's arms.

Just then, Mister Brick came into the room.

When he saw Missy Violet, he got all shamefaced and mealy-mouthed. Just the same, he asked her to name the twins. She named the little girl Safronia, and the sickly little boy she named Samson after the man in the Bible because she said she hoped he'd grow up to be big and strong just like Samson. But she didn't offer Mister Brick a drink of blackberry wine from her flask, the way she did some of the fathers who'd just had a new baby.

And whenever she saw him at church she'd say, "Joe Brick, you gettin' on my bad side. When you gonna pay me my money? This ain't no charity farm you lookin' at here. Now pay up or give me all my babies back!" Because that's the way she would do the fathers who took too long paying her her fee.

Mister Joe Brick never did pay Missy Violet for delivering his children.

MISS NULA IRISH AND JAMES HENRY

ALL OF US CHILDREN LIKED TO PLAY "CHURCH," especially my cousin Charles because he liked to mock the preacher. Sometimes he'd be the Methodist preacher and walk across the yard real slow, with his head bowed and his hands behind his back, mumbling something under his breath just the way Reverend Mims did in the pulpit every Sunday morning before he began his sermon. No one ever heard what Reverend Mims was mumbling, but Charles said he heard him once saying,

"Ooka dooka, soda crackery, do your pappy chew tobacckey."

But the most fun of all was when Charles did Reverend Fletcher, the preacher over at the Baptist church, because the Baptists were more lively than us Methodists. And Charles would squall real loud and slide across the yard with one hand raised in the air and the other one on his hip, shouting, "Glory! Glory! Glory!" And the rest of us would clap and sing, until one of us, usually me, would fall on the ground and all the other children would gather around and fan me until Charles came over and pronounced me "saved." Then we'd all sing "This Little Light of Mine" and church would be over.

One day, Miss Nula Irish, the nosiest and meanest woman in town, walked up on us playing church. Charles was mocking Reverend Fletcher, holding a big white handkerchief in his hand, dipping and sliding across the backyard. Miss Nula went and told Papa. I think it tickled Papa, but Mama thought it was a crying shame and gave Charles a whipping and the rest of us "a good talking to" about "playin' with the Lord" and "mockin' his servants." Charles was hopping mad and made up his mind to get back at Miss Nula for telling. I made things worse by telling him that Miss Nula was going around saying that she didn't like Missy Violet.

Miss Nula had an addle-brained son named James Henry, and he used to plow their field down by the edge of the woods. One day Charles hid behind some trees and called James Henry's name real loud through a bottle gourd. "JAMES HEN-RYYY, THIS THE LORD! THIS THE DAY I CALLS YOU TO PREACH. GO PREACH, JAMES HENRY, GO PREACH!"

Poor James Henry dropped his plow and fell to his knees, and from that day on James Henry Irish thought the Lord had called him to preach. That was a mean thing for Charles to do, and it was kind of sad too, because James Henry couldn't read or write, so he couldn't get his speeches from the Good Book. But he would stand up in church and make up things to say and people would laugh behind his back. Miss Nula was pleased as punch, though, and nobody could tell her the Lord hadn't called her boy to preach.

But Miss Nula's field lay fallow for three months because James Henry refused to plow. All he wanted to do was preach. He wouldn't go out to the field, and when and if he did, he wouldn't plow. He'd just stand there next to the plow and preach to the trees on the edge of the field. He'd stand out in the hot sun all day long until Miss Nula had to go get Papa and Uncle Tom Thomason to bring him in.

I began to feel bad about James Henry and Miss Nula, so I tried to get Charles to tell Papa what he had done, so Papa could straighten things out with Miss Nula and James Henry. But Charles said he didn't give a darn if Miss Nula starved to death. I told him that if he didn't say something to Papa, I'd go to Papa myself, and that's when he said he'd tell Mama I had dipped some of Miss Ida Bean's snuff the last time we went up to her house.

"But you told me to!" I said. "You told me to put a little bit on my tongue, to see if it was sweet."

"Yeah," said Charles, "but I didn't tell you to stuff your whole bottom lip with it and mock Miss Ida. That was your idea." Charles had me over a barrel. What was I going to do? Then I remembered something Missy Violet had taught me about herb medicine. "You got to pick the right tea for the right fever for it to work," she'd told me. So I had to pick the right "comeuppance" for Charles to get him to do the right thing. I thought and thought, then I said, "If you don't go to Papa, I'm gonna tell Arma Jean Pettegrue that you still wet the bed."

That did it. Charles was sweet on Arma Jean, and he would rather have been kicked in the head by a mule than have her know he couldn't hold his water. So Charles went to Papa, but it was too late to stop James Henry from preaching. He preached for the rest of his life and Miss Nula had to hire a man to plow her field, but nobody could tell her James Henry hadn't been called by the Lord to preach.

Mister Som Grit

THE SUMMER I WORKED FOR MISSY VIOLET, MY BIG sister Savanah tried to teach me how to sew. Savanah loved sewing, and she was good at it too. She could make the teeniest, tiniest stitches you ever saw. And they were straight too, straight as arrows. But I was all thumbs and clumsy. I could never make the stitches tiny enough or straight enough to please her. I didn't relish those ol' sewing lessons at all.

"Why do I have to make the stitches so small?" I'd complain to Savanah.

"You want to be a fine seamstress like Mama,

don't you?" she'd ask and I'd say, "Uh-huh," just to be polite. "Then your stitches have to be practically invisible," she'd explain, and make me pull out every last stitch.

"But I wanna learn how to knit, not sew," I'd whine. "I wanna make warm things for the babies Missy Violet's gonna catch this winter while I'm in school."

"Then sewing will help make your fingers nimble," Savanah would say and make me start all over again.

Missy Violet thought it was the sweetest thing she'd ever heard of, when she found out what I wanted to do. "Viney, you are my best helper girl!" she said and gave me a big hug. A few Saturdays later, Missy Violet invited me to her house for a knitting lesson. And since Papa had sent Charles home for the weekend to visit his folks, she said I could bring Arma Jean Pettiegrue along for company. Arma Jean was my best friend—she was a lot of fun, real talky and bold.

But when Arma Jean and I got to Missy Violet's, we were surprised to see a shiny black Packard automobile sitting in her front yard, with a portly man in a derby sitting behind the wheel. "Who's that?" Arma Jean asked.

"That's Mister Som Grit," I whispered. "I think he's sweet on Missy Violet."

"Sugar foot!" Arma Jean squawked and we raced in the house to tell Missy Violet she had a gentleman caller. "Oh, fiddlesticks," she said when she peeped through the curtains and saw the big black Packard sitting in the yard. "It's that widow man from over in Little River. I don't have time for him today, and if he gets in the house, I'll never get rid of him," Missy Violet said and rushed out to the car.

"Why he coming here to see you?" Arma Jean blurted out on the way to the car. Like she didn't like the idea of Mister Som Grit coming by to see Missy Violet.

"Oh, he's just a lonely widow man. We sit on the porch sometimes and talk," Missy Violet explained.

"He sweet on you?" Arma Jean asked and I put my face in my hands, I was so embarrassed. I would never have had the gumption to get in grownups' business the way Arma Jean did. But that was Arma Jean, bold as sunshine!

"You certainly are full of questions and comments this mornin', young lady," Missy Violet scolded. "Now, save something to say for when you die." Arma Jean looked shamefaced and stopped asking questions, and Missy Violet took us over to the car to meet Mister Som Grit.

"He looks like a stack of pancakes wearing a derby," Arma Jean whispered as Mister Som Grit got out of his car. "Afternoon, Mister Grit," Missy Violet said and Mister Grit tipped his big brown derby.

"How you be this fine afternoon, Miss Violet?" Mister Grit asked in a big gruff voice.

"He sounds like a freight train, don't he?" Arma Jean whispered, and we both snickered.

"I'm doing tolerable, thank you," Missy Violet answered politely. "And you?"

Mister Som Grit reared back and grinned a great big wide grin. "Well, I suspect I'm doin' mighty fine, now that I done laid eyes on you, Miss Violet," he cooed.

A surprised look came over Missy Violet's face, and her cheeks turned dark and rosy and she smiled a little crooked smile, like the one our schoolteacher, Miss Glover, smiles when one of the children says something out of the way. "Why, you silver-tongued devil, you," Missy Violet said and patted her hair.

"How'd you like to go for a ride in my automobile?" Mister Grit asked and flashed another big ol' toothy grin at Missy Violet.

"I'm terribly sorry, Mister Grit, but I promised these girls a knitting lesson this afternoon," Missy Violet told him.

Mister Som Grit's face fell like a theater curtain, and he shot me and Arma Jean a hard look. "Well," he said, in his big rough voice, "I reckon I could just come inside and set a spell." And before Missy Violet could say a word, he'd hauled himself inside and plopped down on the settee in Missy Violet's parlor.

"I do declare, Miss Violet," he said, "I sho' could use a helpin' of your fine peach cobbler right about now." Lordy, how did he know Missy Violet had made peach cobbler?

Mister Som Grit wolfed down three pieces of Missy Violet's delicious peach cobbler, then reared back and patted his big long stomach. "You a fine cook, Miss Violet, a mighty fine cook, indeed," he sighed.

"Glad you enjoyed it," Missy Violet said, "but I'm goin' to have to excuse myself now and give these girls their knitting lesson. Won't have time to sit and chat today."

Mister Grit looked let down, but he didn't budge. "Don't let me bother y'all none," he insisted and, like a screech owl, closed his eyes for a nap.

When Missy Violet left the parlor to get the knitting yarn, Arma Jean said, "We'll fix him," and ran over by the settee and pretended to fall over one of Mister Grit's big foots, then accidentally-on-purpose she poked him with one of Missy Violet's knitting needles. "YOW!" Som Grit squalled. Then Arma Jean sat on his derby. Mister Grit gave Arma Jean a mean look, but he still sat right there, just like a bump on a log.

When Missy Violet came back into the parlor, Mister Grit winked at her. "Oooooh, did you see that?" Arma Jean whispered. But before I could answer and before she could get her hands on Missy Violet's knitting needle to give Mister Som Grit another good poke, somebody knocked on the door and spoiled the whole afternoon for all of us.

Miss Pula Dash stood at the door. When Missy Violet saw her, a kind of frightened, angry look came over her face. Nobody wanted anything to do with Pula Dash. Folks said she was a witch and could make people sick, or make them yelp like a dog or stick to the wall like a magnet. No one ever went to her house unless they had business with the devil.

"What can I do for you, Pula?" Missy Violet asked calmly as Miss Pula walked in the room. She was a curious-looking lady, kind of smallish, with one shoulder higher than the other. But the most peculiar things about her were her skin and eyes. Her skin was beige-colored and saggy, even though she wasn't old. And her eyes were gold like a cat's and very, very tiny. The tiniest eyes I'd ever seen. Smaller than a shrimp's eyes.

"My gal's time done come," Miss Pula said to Missy Violet and went back out the door.

"For God's sake, you ain't goin', is you, Violet?" Mister Som Grit whispered in a shaky voice, but Missy Violet was already getting her bag. "You not scared?" Mister Grit asked.

"Well, I'm not faint-hearted, if that's what you mean. And I don't hold with the likes of Pula Dash and her kind," Missy Violet answered. "But I'm goin' with the Almighty's name on my lips and with my birthin' bag in my hand to see if I can help that poor child. It's not her fault her mama's a conjure woman," Missy Violet said and took a deep breath. "Will you drive me out there?" we heard her ask Mister Grit as she walked through the door.

Mister Grit scratched his head. "Oh, Lordy!" we heard him say, but he went on outside and started up the car.

"Come on, children, we got a call to make," Missy Violet said and Arma Jean and I followed her to the car.

Mister Grit drove slow and talked all the way. He had gotten some of his wind back and his voice was loud like a freight train again. "Violet, ain't you scared she might put some kind of spell on you?" he asked.

"Now, why would she do a thing like that?" Missy

Violet replied. "Why would she put a spell on the person who's coming to help her?"

"'Cause she mean, that's why! Mean as a rattlesnake," Mister Som Grit answered. "You heard what she done to Covington Brown! Put a stumble and fall curse on him. Poor fella', can't walk more than half a mile without stumblin' and fallin'. And they say she don't eat nothin' but cat livers and babies!" When Mister Som Grit said that, Missy Violet made him stop the car, and she told him something that made him straighten up and behave like a citizen.

"Now, I can't tolerate you if you don't have no backbone," she said. "This here's a woman that needs tendin' to, and I'm her neighbor and I got to help her. It's none of my business what she do the rest of the year. Now do you want me and these children to get out and walk the rest of the way so you can run home and get up under the bed like an old woman, or you going to take us out there?"

Mister Grit's mouth fell open, then a sheepish look came on his face for a minute and big beads of sweat popped out on his forehead. "Look at him," Arma Jean whispered, "he ain't nothin' but a big ol' scaredy-cat."

But Mister Grit mopped his brow with a big white handkerchief and turned to Missy Violet and assured her in his big freight train voice, "Now Miss Violet, I'll have you know, I ain't no piddlin' man. I got plenty-a backbone. I just wanted to be sure you wanted to go out there yourself, that's all!" Then the car jerked off and we were on our way, down to the deep part of the woods everybody called The Bottoms.

THE ZENOBIA TREE

THE BOTTOMS WAS IN THE DEEP-IN-THE-DARK PART of the woods. Lots of weeping willow trees and tangled up vines hung across the road. It might have been pretty down there if it hadn't been so spooky. There was no driving road leading to Pula Dash's house, so Mister Grit had to let us out at a footpath and we walked the rest of the way while he waited in the car. The house was just an old shack, and Pula Dash was sitting outside on the steps when we came. She got up and went inside when she saw us. "Stay out here, children," Missy Violet warned, before Arma Jean and I could slip inside.

But as soon as the door closed behind them, Arma Jean grabbed my arm and hissed, "Come on!" She pulled me around to the side of the cabin. "Where we goin'?" I asked.

"Window!" she pointed and pulled me to a boarded-up window on the side of the cabin. Arma Jean stuck her head under one of the loose boards.

"What you see?" I asked.

"Come, look," Arma Jean said, and I poked my head up near hers. It was very dark inside, and even though it was daytime a candle flickered on a table next to a cot. A teenage girl was lying there next to a small bundle. Missy Violet picked up the little bundle and shook her head. "It's too late, Pula," she said. "It's dead." Then she handed the bundle to Miss Pula. Pula's face went hard like a stone. We thought she was going to put some kind of spell on Missy Violet. "Why didn't you come for me sooner?

Maybe I could have helped this baby or helped your girl." Miss Pula didn't answer, just stared at the floor. All of a sudden she didn't look so scary anymore, just sad.

Missy Violet bathed the little dead baby and wrapped her in one of the nice clean receiving blankets she had in her bag, then Miss Pula put the baby in a shoebox and handed it back to Missy Violet. "You take care of this for me, Violet," Miss Pula said.

"Have you named her?" Missy Violet asked.

"Zenobia, after her mama," Miss Pula answered.

Then Miss Pula and Missy Violet bathed the girl lying on the cart and wrapped her in a sheet. "Should I send the undertaker?" Missy Violet asked, and Miss Pula Dash nodded her head. Missy Violet carried the shoebox with her out to the car. Arma Jean and I pretended we had been sitting on the steps the whole time. "Come along, children," she said.

When we got back to the car, Missy Violet set the shoebox on the front seat between her and Mister

Grit. Mister Grit's eyes almost popped out of his head, but he didn't say a word. Arma Jean and I were very quiet too. I guess we were both thinking about what we saw in Miss Pula's house.

It wasn't the first time I'd seen a dead person. Mister Joe White, the postmaster, was the first dead person I'd ever laid eyes on. When the white Methodist Church wouldn't let the colored folks in for Mister White's funeral, Miss Betty, his wife, wouldn't let the gravediggers bury him until all the colored people and their children had marched around his casket at the grave for the last look. And that was because the colored people of Richmond County said Mister Joe was the best white man who ever put on a shoe, and they loved him and Miss Betty. But I had never seen a dead *young* person or baby before. The next thing I knew I was gripping Arma Jean's wrist and she was gripping mine.

"I couldn't help them. It was too late," we heard Missy Violet say. And before we got back to the house, she had Mister Grit stop the car by a beautiful tree dripping with magnolia blossoms and honeysuckle vines. Later, Arma Jean and I named it "the Zenobia tree." It was our little secret.

Missy Violet made us stay in the car while she and Mister Grit went behind the tree. We couldn't see what they were doing, but, when they came back they didn't have the shoebox anymore. And I remember Missy Violet saying to Mister Grit on the way back home, "With all her conjurin', she couldn't do a thing to save her own kin."

Mister Som Grit made himself scarce at Missy Violet's house after that, and we finally got to our knitting lessons. But I don't think any of us was as afraid of Miss Pula Dash as we had been because we knew now she didn't have any special powers over death.

First Sunday

My Papa was a good man, but he wasn't a church-going man, and sometimes he and Mama had words over this.

Mama thought it was scandalous if a man didn't attend church every Sunday with his family. Papa said reading the Good Book was good enough for him. Mama said he still needed to show his face in the church door more often. But Papa said, "You can't measure a man's uprightness by the amount of singin' he do at the church." Then Mama said Papa needed to set a better example for his children and that made Papa angry and he said Mama "got so much religion, she want to have Sunday every day." Then Mama started quoting scripture and Papa started holding his head. And they passed words back and forth like that until they came to a truce and Papa agreed to attend church with the family every first Sunday of the month.

Mama was pleased as punch, because First Sunday was Communion Sunday, and practically all of Richmond County showed up on Communion Sunday and they would get to see Papa worshiping with his family.

So when the next First Sunday rolled around, Mama had all of us children polished and shining in our Sunday-go-to-meeting clothes. Papa wore his dark suit and put on his gray felt hat. Mama wore her good pearls, the ones Papa gave her when they first got married.

The church was already crowded inside when we

got there, but Mama spied some empty seats up near the front and strutted right up to the front row. Papa hung back to let Mama know he didn't relish sitting up front. But Mama gave Papa a hard look and he came on up to the front-row pew. I think Mama was just so proud to have Papa at church with us that she wanted everybody to see him there.

Sitting across the aisle from us were the Pooles. I tried to smile at Margie Poole, but she rolled her eyes at me and stuck out her leg so I could see she was wearing cotton stockings and new patent-leather slippers with bright shiny buckles on the side. I just pretended I didn't see them and looked up in the choir loft until the organ sounded and the choir stood up to sing. Savior Brown sang "Old Ship of Zion" and Mama leaned over and asked Papa if he was enjoying the singing. Papa said he was enjoying it "just fine."

"That girl's throat must be made of pure gold," Mama said to Papa, and Papa nodded. We made a pretty picture that morning, sitting there in the front-row pew, Papa holding baby Cleo on his lap, Mama looking up at Papa, all happy and proud. Savanah and me in our yellow organza dresses and our four brothers in their brown suits. All worshiping together at the Methodist A.M.E. Church. Papa had settled back in his seat and was enjoying the sermon. I could tell he was enjoying it because he kept nodding his head—then something happened and Papa never set foot in that church again.

A traveling preacher was visiting our church that morning, and he was stirring up the congregation pretty good. And that was amazing because Mama always said it would take something akin to an earthquake to stir up a Methodist church. But that morning, all the settled ladies sitting in the Amen Corner had started fanning, and I could see Missy Violet nodding her head in agreement with the preacher. And Miss Mattie Ruth Corn kept squallin',

"Amen! Amen!" every time the preacher got in a good lick for the Lord against the devil. And Deacon Rufus Bell had started patting his foot.

All of a sudden, a strange man stood up in the congregation and accused the traveling preacher of sullying his daughter's good name. He said the preacher had promised to marry his daughter, when he was already married with six children. Then the man drew a pistol and POW! POW! POW!

It was like the whole congregation exploded! Folks started screaming and running, ducking under pews. Poor Reverend Mims struck his head on a piano leg, trying to get under the piano stool, and knocked himself out. The traveling preacher almost broke his leg jumping out the church window. But he was able to limp to his automobile and get away.

Mama was crying and praying and, Papa kept shouting for all of us to stay underneath the front-row pew. Finally some deacons wrestled the man with the pistol to the floor. Later on we found out his name was Saxton Jacks and he was from Winston-Salem, North Carolina, and that what he had said about the traveling preacher was true.

Mama was so ashamed, she cried all day after we got back home and kept asking how such an ugly thing could happen in the Lord's house. And Papa kept saying, "Didn't I tell you old Satan love to dodge around amongst the crowd at the Sunday meetin'?"

Not long after Saxton Jacks ruined church for my mama, Missy Violet and some of the other ladies from the church came around to comfort her. They told her to stop fretting over what had happened on First Sunday and be glad that the devil was run out from among the flock. They said it right in front of Papa too, and Missy Violet said she agreed with what Papa said about the devil lovin' to skirt around at the church meetings. "Didn't he go right up in heaven and get in amongst God's holy angels?" Missy Violet reminded us.

"Amen, he sure did! It say so right in the Book of Job," Missus Arbadella Queen pointed out.

"He slide in there late too," added Miss Doretha, and all the ladies agreed.

"So it's nothin' if he tend church with us once in a while, child," Missy Violet told Mama. Mama felt better after they left, and she didn't bother Papa about going to church for a while, but she never stopped hoping he'd come back on his own, and he did. But he went to the Baptists. He never set foot in the Methodist A.M.E. Church of Richmond County again.

THE DAY I WAS BORN

TODAY MISSY VIOLET TOLD ME ABOUT THE DAY I came into the world. She said it was around harvest time and the gypsies had come to town and were camping out in the pine tree grove behind Mister Claude Davies's house. That morning, some of them had come up into Missy Violet's yard to ask for water from her well. Most folks back then didn't let gypsies on their property because they didn't trust them. Some would even turn the dogs on them, said they'd "steal the shortenin' out a biscuit" if you didn't keep your eye on them. But Missy Violet said she always allowed them to get water from her well because everybody needed some water and because a lot of the mean things people said about gypsies were just made-up stories, like some of the mean things people said about colored people.

So the gypsies were still in the yard getting water from Missy Violet's well when Papa rode up on his horse hollering that Mama's time had come. Missy Violet got her bag and got on the horse with Papa and came to the house to see Mama. But Missy Violet said after she'd been with Mama for about an hour, here come Mister Hubert Clifford riding up in our yard, looking for Missy Violet. He said the time had come for his wife, Effie, too.

Missy Violet said Miss Effie was one of her rich, well-to-do white ladies, and she was very skittish and hard to please. And even though she could have afforded any doctor in the county, Effie wanted Missy Violet to deliver her baby. I laughed when Missy Violet told how, in the months before her baby was born, Miss Effie used to chase Mister

Clifford out of the house and throw things at his head and refuse to let him back in until he'd brought Missy Violet back with him.

Missy Violet said she would go to the house and find Miss Effie all in a tizzy, crying and holding her head and throwing things at poor Mister Clifford. Mister Clifford was so afraid she was going to hurt herself or the child if she didn't calm down. "Now it won't do for you to fall apart too," Missy Violet would tell Mister Clifford and pat him on the shoulder. Then she'd go inside the house and try to calm Miss Effie down.

"Child, why you takin' on so?" Missy Violet would ask, and Miss Effie would complain to Missy Violet that her dresses were getting too tight, her ankles were swollen, and that Mister Clifford wasn't giving her enough attention. "Look at me!" she'd screech. "I look like a prize pig at the fair! I hate being in a family way!"

Missy Violet said she would have to get real firm with Miss Effie then. "Child, quiet yourself!" she'd say. "I'm surprised at you carryin' on like this, a young lady with your upbringin'." Then Missy Violet would tell her, "Come sit here by me and tell me what ails you." And Miss Effie would sob into her hankie and tell Missy Violet that she didn't want to have a baby and that she didn't know how other women went through such a thing.

Missy Violet said she would let Effie talk and talk before telling her, "You know, you was difficult when I attended your birth, and I see I'm gonna have trouble with you now." Then Missy Violet showed me how she would press her lips together and make a mean face while she was talking so Miss Effie would get the point. It reminded me of the way Mama sometimes pressed her lips together and made a mean face at Papa whenever he said something out of the way about the preacher.

Missy Violet said Miss Effie would look real sheepish after that and moan, "Oh, Missy Violet, what's wrong with me?"

"You just scared, child," Missy Violet would tell

her and stroke her hair. "That's all, you just scared."
And then she'd fix Miss Effie a cup of comfrey tea
and pat cold compresses on her head and wrists and
feel her belly to make sure the baby was all right.
Then she'd call Mister Clifford in and make him a
cup of tea too, and while he sipped it she'd get Miss
Effie settled in bed.

Missy Violet said it was because of all this courtesy
and because she had attended Miss Effie's birth and
the birth of Miss Effie's sisters and brothers, and
because Miss Effie's family had once owned Missy
Violet's family back in slavery time, that Miss Effie
felt like she owned Missy Violet. Missy Violet said
sometimes she would have to remind Miss Effie that
they weren't living back in the olden days anymore.
"Now, young lady, Missy Violet's a free citizen now.
She not your family's sole property anymore, and
she free to see after her other ladies whenever she
wants to," Missy Violet would remind her.

So on that day when I was born, Missy Violet had

to tell Mister Clifford to go on back home because I was about ready to come into the world, and since Mama was on her sixth baby she would deliver sooner than Miss Effie, who was a first-time mother. So Mister Clifford, who was a rich man but never acted like it, and wore overalls and always laughed and talked with the colored folks, went on home, and twenty minutes later I was born.

Later on that same day, Mister Clifford's baby daughter, Eleanor, also came into the world, and Mister Clifford was so excited that a little colored baby and a little white baby had been born on the same day, in the same county, delivered by the same midwife, that he came out to the house and asked Papa if he could give me his baby daughter's middle name. Papa felt honored and said he could, so that's why my name is Viney Eleanor and Mister Hubert Clifford's daughter is named Suzy Eleanor, and why Papa and Mister Clifford always stop and shake hands whenever they meet.

VINEY SAVES THE DAY

NOT LONG AFTER SCHOOL STARTED MISSY VIOLET went down to Florida to visit her brother. "Now, you be good in school, mind your teacher, and get your lessons out," she instructed me before she left. "And if you get good grades this year, Missy Violet'll see about you workin' with her next summer. I need a good helper like you," she said, and she gave me a big hug.

I was sad when Missy Violet left, but I was glad to be back in school. I liked school and I liked my teacher, Miss Glover. Besides, I really had something special to write about this year when the time came for us to do essays on what we did over the summer. I had learned how babies came into the world! That was something even some big girls didn't know. Not only that, but I had learned the names of different roots and herbs and what they were good for. If I had to, I could make an onion poultice for boils or a good headache liniment from cayenne peppers. I also knew what special teas Missy Violet brewed for her ladies in childbirth labor. I could even recognize them in the woods and in the fields.

Not long after Missy Violet left for Florida, my cousin Charles came back from Mt. Gilead to go to school. His papa had taken him up north over the summer to visit some relatives in New York City, and that was all he could talk about. At first it was fun hearing about the skyscrapers and the trolley cars and the trains that run underground, but then it got to be like a mosquito buzzing in our ears.

Besides, Charles got all puffed-up and nobody could stand to be around him. You'd think he had been all over the world, the way he carried on.

Mama tried to get Charles to talk about something else one evening at the supper table. "Charles," she said, very politely, "how you coming along with your schoolwork?"

"Just fine, ma'am," Charles boomed, and began bragging about what a smart fella he was and how he was sure to win the essay contest with his story about his trip up to New York City. Mama looked across the table at Papa for help.

"Let him talk, Lena," Papa said. "At least while he's talkin' he's not stirrin' up mischief." So Charles talked on and on. But something happened a few weeks after that that gave *me* something to talk about.

One day Charles and I were walking home from school when we passed by Miss Betty White's house. Miss Betty was sitting on the porch with her daughter-in-law. Not the snooty one from Connecticut who was married to her oldest son, Robert, but the one from Birmingham, Alabama, who was married to her youngest son, John. We stopped and talked to Miss Betty for a few minutes, and she introduced us to her daughter-in-law. Her name was Peggy and she was going to have a baby. Miss Betty said she would soon be returning home to Birmingham so she could have her baby with her mama by her side.

A few days later, Miss Betty sent word to Mama for me to come over to her house right away. I thought Miss Betty had some fresh churned butter to send to Mama, but when I got there I found out that her daughter-in-law's time had come.

"Viney, I understand you helped Missy Violet catch babies this past summer," Miss Betty said.

"Yes, ma'am," I answered, but the bottom of my stomach dropped out when she said that, because

Missy Violet was out of town. I wondered what Miss Betty expected *me* to do!

"You sit here with Peggy while John and I go fetch Doctor Parker," Miss Betty announced and walked out the door with Mister John. Peggy was sitting in the middle of a big iron bed in Betty's bedroom. She looked very pale and nervous, but she wasn't moaning and groaning yet. She tried to smile. "A young girl like you know how to catch babies?" she asked.

"Sort of, ma'am," I answered. It felt funny calling her "ma'am" because she didn't look much older than my sister Savanah. "Missy Violet does most of the work," I told her. "I just do what I'm told, mostly." I thought about Missy Violet and asked myself what she would do if she were there. Most likely she'd say some kind words to Miss Peggy and fluff up her pillows. So I said, "Don't be afraid, Miss Peggy. I'm here to help you." Then I fluffed her pillows. I hadn't said it exactly the way Missy Violet would have, but I'd said some kind words to her and I thought Missy Violet would have been proud of me. She always said that it was very, very important to speak kind words to sick people and to ladies giving birth. She said the kind words were like a dose of strong medicine.

"Your mama have a lot of children?" Miss Peggy asked.

"Yes, ma'am."

"How many?" she wanted to know.

"Seven," I told her.

"You must know a lot about babies, then," she said.

"Well, most of what I know I learned from Missy Violet," I explained. "She's the one who taught me how to make expecting mothers comfortable. She even taught me how to give a back rub. Missy Violet's famous for her back rubs. She says sometimes a back rub can help you bear the pains better. Would you like for me to give you a rub? I can do it just like she taught me, moving my hands around in circles, up and down your spine, pressing like I'm kneading dough."

"That sounds good to me," Miss Peggy said. "I'm starting to feel awful bad." So I got up on the bed and rubbed her back. While I rubbed I taught her a little song that she could sing to her baby when it was born:

> *Roses on my shoulders,*
> *Slippers on my feet,*
> *I'm my mama's darlin',*
> *Don't you think I'm sweet.*

"You got good hands, Viney," Miss Peggy said as I rubbed. "You'll make a good midwife someday." When Miss Peggy told me that, I got a warm feeling inside. Just imagine—*me* a midwife someday! Maybe I could do it. I had learned a lot from Missy Violet and was looking forward to learning more. I wasn't afraid of sick people anymore, or of women who were going to have babies. Now I wanted to help them and I knew how. Maybe I didn't know how to "catch" a baby yet, but I did know how to comfort people.

Just as I was finishing Miss Peggy's back rub, Miss Betty and Mister John burst through the door. The Doctor Parker was not with them. Miss Betty was wringing her hands. "Dear Lord, what are we going to do? There's not a doctor anywhere, not even in the next county."

"They're all up in Washington at some medical convention," Mister John sputtered.

Miss Betty rushed over to the bed and took a look at Miss Peggy and patted her cheek. "How you coming along, child?" she asked Miss Peggy with a worried look on her face.

"I'm beginnin' to feel awful, awful bad, Mother White," Miss Peggy answered. Miss Betty looked at me. *What would Missy Violet do now?* I wondered. *Tea. She would give her tea,* I thought. But I didn't have any of Missy Violet's special teas with me. "Do you have any kind of tea in the house, Miss Betty?" I asked.

"Just some plain tea and some peppermint tea," she answered. Well, it wouldn't be the same as one of Missy Violet's special teas, but I remembered her saying that peppermint tea was good for most anything. So I asked Miss Betty to make Miss Peggy a cup of hot peppermint tea. While she made the tea, Mister John and I got Miss Peggy out of bed and walked her back and forth across the floor. It wasn't long before she was moaning and groaning.

"Do you know anyone else who can help us?" Miss Betty asked when she came back into the room. I thought and thought, but no one came to mind. Maybe I would just have to run home and get Mama? Then a light clicked on in my head. I remembered Missy Violet used to talk about another midwife who lived a few counties away. A lady by the name of Annie McLeod.

"I know, I know!" I shouted. "Miss Annie McLeod in Rockingham!"

It was a long ride, but that was the only other midwife I knew of. So Miss Betty's son and I drove to Rockingham in Miss Betty's car. When we got there, Mister John drove up to the first person he saw, an old farmer in overalls. "Do you know a Miss Annie McLeod?" he asked the old farmer.

The farmer pushed his cap back and scratched his head. "Well, now, we got a couple of Annie McLeods around here. Which one you want?"

"The midwife," Mister John said.

"Well, in that case you got to go over yonder behind the sawmill," the farmer said and pointed up a dirt road.

"Somebody fixin' to have a baby?" he called after us as Mister John drove off.

About a mile up the road on the other side of the sawmill we came to a small house. It wasn't cheerful-looking with pretty flowers growing in front like Missy Violet's house was, but it was as neat as a pin. A thin lady wearing spectacles and a straw hat the color of roasted coffee was sitting on the porch.

Mister John called to her from the car. "You Annie McLeod the midwife?"

"Who want to know?" the lady snapped.

"I do, ma'am. My name is John White. I drove all the way down here from Mangum to find a midwife. My wife's time come early, and the midwife and the doctor are both out of town."

"Mangum? You come all the way down here from Mangum?"

"Yes, ma'am. Drove all the way down here on the recommendation of this little girl here." The midwife looked at me and frowned. "This is Viney," Mister John said.

"I don't know no Viney," Annie McLeod snapped.

"Are you acquainted with Miss Violet McCrae?"

"I am," the midwife answered. "But I don't

know this young gal," she said and leaned forward in her rocking chair to give me a hard look. The kind of displeased look people give my cousin Charles sometimes.

"I'll see that you get double your fee and a ride back home," Mister John told her. The midwife pressed her lips together and made a face, the kind of face Mama made sometimes when one of us children started to get on her nerve. Then she got up from her rocker and headed for the front door. "Let me get my satchel," she said.

By the time we got back to Miss Betty's house, the baby was ready to be born. I told Miss Annie I could get behind the pillows and help Miss Peggy push if she needed me to. She looked at me over her spectacles. "Umph! Is that so?" she said, and kept on digging in her satchel.

"I learned that from being Missy Violet's helper girl," I explained. But Miss Annie didn't answer, just kept on doing what she was doing. But she did let me stay in the room when she put Miss Betty and Mister John out into the hall because Miss Betty couldn't stop talking and Mister John had turned snow white.

Miss Annie McLeod was much older than Missy Violet. Her hands were rough and leathery-looking, and she moved around like she was made of wood. And she had her own way of doing things too, her own way of getting the mother to push the baby out. "Girl, this baby ain't gonna ride out here on no chariot. You got to help him come out," she told Miss Peggy.

Poor Miss Peggy, she was already plumb tuckered out. "Somebody help me, please!" she cried.

So to show Miss Annie I knew my beans I said, "Do you want me to lie across her belly, ma'am?"

"You stay in a child's place, gal," Miss Annie snapped at me. But when she saw I was still going to stay in the room, even after she'd told me to stay in my place, she said, "Well, since you so determined to have a hand in this, get up behind those pillows and help her push." So I climbed up on the bed and got behind Miss Peggy.

"Come on, Miss Peggy, you can do it. I'll help you," I said. Miss Peggy pushed and I pushed and Miss Annie kept barking at us like an army sergeant.

"Is that all the strength you two got? Push! Bear down hard, girl! I don't wanna be here till Judgment Day!" So between her bossing and us pushing, Miss Annie McLeod worked her midwife magic and the three of us soon brought a brand-new baby into the world.

"What you wanna name this boy?" Miss Annie asked as she held the squalling baby up by his little feet.

"It's a boy? Oh, let me hold him, please," Miss Peggy begged, and Miss Annie cleaned the baby up and handed him to his mother. He was all red and wrinkly. "He's so beautiful," Miss Peggy cooed when she saw him.

Miss Annie went to the door and gave Miss Betty

and Mister John the good news while Miss Betty burst into tears. "Oh, John, how I wish your father was here," she cried. Then she rushed over to see the baby. I thought Mister John would burst wide open with pride over his son. He couldn't stop thanking his wife and saying sweet things to her.

"Miss Annie, do you want me to put the stamp on the envelope so you can mail the birth record to the county seat?" I asked to let Miss Annie know I really knew all about midwifing.

"Violet trained you good, didn't she?" she said and almost gave me a smile. And she let me put the stamp on the envelope.

After everything had quieted down and Miss Peggy and the new baby, who they named Joseph after Miss Betty's dead husband, were fast asleep, Miss Betty went into the dining room and brought out a fancy glass filled with strawberry cordial. She handed it to Miss Annie, and Miss Annie threw her head back and swallowed it straight down. Mister

John shook Miss Annie's hand and paid her the double fee he had promised her and got ready to drive her back to Rockingham.

Before she got in the car she looked at me over her spectacles again and said, "You done good, little gal."

Miss Betty bragged to everybody in the neighborhood, both colored and white, about how courageous I had been, how I had saved the day. Everybody at church heard about it. And at school all the girls kept coming up to me, asking me questions about babies and if I'd been scared. Even Margie Poole came up to me. She didn't ask about what happened at Miss Betty's, but she did say she liked my hair ribbons. Even Charles was proud of me. He tried to act like he wasn't, he'd say, "Aw, that wasn't nothin'. Any sissy coulda done that." But then he'd brag to all the boys at school about what his cousin Viney had done for Miss Betty.

Best of all, Missy Violet was so proud of me when she got back. I'd handled myself like a big girl, like somebody with backbone. I wasn't the same silly little girl who thought babies came out of tree stumps and cabbage patches. I was a midwife's helper, and I knew a few things about "catchin'" babies.